Penny and the Captain

Penny and the Captain

TALES AND PICTURES BY
JANE BRESKIN ZALBEN

COLLINS 🌳 WORLD

New York • Cleveland

Library of Congress Cataloging in Publication Data
Zalben, Jane Breskin, Penny and the captain.
CONTENTS: The birthday gift.—The meeting.—
All alone.—The cardgame.—Penny and the captain.
[1. Penguins—Fiction] I. Title.   PZ7.Z254Pe3   [E]   76-54826
ISBN 0-529-05424-8   ISBN 0-529-05425-6 lib. bdg.

ISBN 0-00-184629-9 (U.K.)

To Sandra Jordan, with love and friendship,
for the endless hours of editing
...who knows Penny in her heart.
And to Ann Beneduce who made it possible.

Contents

Mr. Jenkins is a sea captain.
He lives on a sailboat
with his first mate,
Penelope Adelie Willington the Third.
Captain Jenkins calls her Penny.
They have known each other for a long time.
They have seen many seaports together.
These are some stories about them.

The Birthday Gift

⸻◆⸻

Penny's birthday was coming,
and she was homesick.
She missed the games
of tag with her friends,
swimming from iceberg to iceberg.
She remembered walking
on the cold, snowy beach
and jumping from rock to rock.
Penny was so unhappy.

Captain Jenkins sighed,
"She doesn't strut on deck with
her perky, little steps anymore."
So he said to himself, "I'll think
of a very special present."
He thought about Penny's gift
in the morning at breakfast,

in the afternoon smoking his pipe,

and before he went to sleep.

While brushing a tooth,
he shouted, "I've got it!"
"I know just the present she'll love,"
he boasted to the crew.
He wrote a letter to Penny's
Aunt Adeline in the South Pole.

A week later, a big box
came in the mail.
The captain lifted the crate
on the ship.
There was a note on it.

To: Penelope Adelie Willington the Third
       c/o Captain Jenkins
       The Silverfish
From: The South Pole
       First Class
       Special Delivery
The crew watched.
"What is it?"
"It's a secret," he said.
He put five locks
and a big sign on it:
DO NOT OPEN UNTIL
PENNY'S BIRTHDAY.

Captain Jenkins hid
Penny's gift.
Penny was sad on
her birthday morning.
She sobbed,
"I want to go home."
The captain said,
"Before you go,
I have a big
surprise for you."
She followed him
around the deck,
under a sail,
down the ladder,
and into her cabin.
He opened the door.
She peeked eagerly
past the corner.

There was a large wooden crate.
And in the crate was a freezer.
In the freezer was a huge block of ice.
"An iceberg!" cried Penny.
"I'll put it in the bathtub!
This is the best present ever,"
Penny squealed.
She hugged Captain Jenkins.

At her party she told the crew,
"I have an iceberg in *my* bathtub."
No one listened. "Who cares?"
Penny whispered to the captain.

Because that night
she took a bath,
and it felt
just like home.

The Meeting

One time Captain Jenkins and Penny
sailed into the sunny port at Singapore.
"My great Aunt Adeline has left the
cold winds of Antarctica," said Penny.
"I think she's living in
a nearby fishing village."

Penny placed an advertisement
in the newspaper:
Dear Aunt Adeline,
Will be here one week.
Hope to see you soon.
Aboard *The Silverfish*.
Will leave Hong-shor pier
next Tuesday 4 P.M.
Love, Penny.
That night she dreamed of her aunt
joining them on *The Silverfish*
as they sailed around the world.

The following morning,
she waited for hours,
pacing the dock.
She stamped her foot.
"Where is she?"
Penny wandered the streets,
looking and looking.
At last she saw a large crowd.
In the middle of it was a penguin
standing on her head
on a bed of seaweed.

Penny thought,
"This can only be my aunt.
She even looks like me."
"Aunt Addie?" Penny called
over the heads of the crowd.
"Penelope darling,"
called her aunt,
still upside down.
She didn't seem at all surprised
to see her niece,
as if it happened every day.

"Where were you?" Penny cried.

"Omm," hummed Addie, looking up.

"Lately I've been diving for pearls."

Penny smiled. "I just can't
be mad at her. The stories
about her chasing sea leopards,
playing hide and seek with whales,
and throwing snowballs at seals
are probably all true."

"You must come with me,
Penelope, my child."

Penny nodded. "I'd love to."

"But first I want to meet the
famous captain of *The Silverfish*,"
demanded Aunt Addie.

Penny led her aunt to
Captain Jenkins' favorite cafe.

"This is Adeline," said Penny.

Aunt Adeline and Captain Jenkins
liked each other at once.
They all spent a lot of time together.

They dove for oysters
and went deep-sea fishing.

They sipped tea on the floor.
They also **drank rum**.

Addie taught them yoga.
They sang her sea chanteys.

They gazed at the stars
and rowed by moonlight.

The week passed quickly by.
It was Tuesday.
Captain Jenkins begged,
"Addie, sail with us."
Penny added, "I wish
you would come."
Addie thought for a moment.
"You love to sail the rough
seas in all sorts of weather.
I want to dive for pearls
in warm, sunny climates.
And if we could do both together,
that would be wonderful,
but since we can't,
we must go our separate ways."
And so she waved good-bye.

Penny thought she saw a tear
on the captain's cheek
as *The Silverfish* chugged
away from shore,
but she wouldn't
swear to it.

All Alone

Penny and the crew
left *The Silverfish* overnight
to buy bananas, peanuts, and oranges.
Captain Jenkins was all alone.
He watched the dinghy
row toward shore.
"Now I'll get some peace
and quiet," he said.
"I'll do all the things
I want to do."

He stayed under the blanket after dawn
and didn't get dressed right away.

He gargled to the tune of
"Row, Row, Row Your Boat" very loud.

He ate banana-cream pie with
his fingers and didn't use a napkin.

He didn't wear his captain's hat.

He spread his stamp collection
about the whole cabin.
And he left it there.
"This is a really
nice change for me."

The captain strolled
about the deck.
He sat in his armchair.
He got up.
"Penny's looks more comfortable."

He heard a crash.
"Who's there?" he shouted.
No one answered.
Swishing and whistling sounds
floated in the air.
He jumped. "What's that?"
It was the sails blowing.
He made himself
a kettle of soup.
It was too much for one.
He sang songs.
No one hummed or clapped.
He made up a story.
There was nobody to listen.
There wasn't even anyone to say to him,
"Hush up! You're making a racket!"
And there was no one
to laugh at his bad jokes.

It was very still and quiet
as the sun sank behind the sea.
The captain knew that Penny and
the crew wouldn't be home that night.
Still, every five minutes he ran
to see if they were coming.
There was nothing to see for miles.

"It's good to be by yourself,"
he thought, "to have a good time
with yourself, but it is also
fun to be with good friends."
He hated to admit it,
but he missed them very much
with all their noise and chatter.

When Penny and the crew returned,
Penny asked, "Did you have a nice time?"
The captain said, "I was so busy
I didn't even think about you."
Penny turned around and
saw him wink at the crew.

She gave him a poke
and said, "Oh, you!"
And they all ate
leftover soup for lunch
for a whole week!

The Card Game

"Do you want to play cards?"
asked Captain Jenkins.
"OK," said Penny.
"Let's play Go Fish," said the captain.
"But I have to tell you
I am really good."
"How do you play?" asked Penny.
The captain taught Penny.
They played for peanuts.

Penny won the first game.
"Beginner's luck,"
mumbled Captain Jenkins.
Penny won the second one, too.
The captain became restless.
They played for a third time,
and after a few minutes,
Penny shouted "Ha, I've won!"
"I thought you didn't know how
to play," yelled Captain Jenkins.
"I don't," snapped Penny.
"I just love peanuts.
So I tried very hard."
"I'll see you later,"
said Captain Jenkins.
"I'm out of peanuts."
"Oh, let's play more," nudged Penny.
"I'll give you some of mine."

"I don't feel like playing any more.
I'm going to sit alone."
Penny felt bad.
And lonely.
So did the captain.

She wanted to make up.
"It's fun to win, but not nice
to rub it in," she thought.
"Would you like some peanuts?
I even took the shells off."

"Oh, all right,"
muttered Captain Jenkins.
He added, "I'm sorry
I was a bad loser."
Penny said, "Let's forget it.
Do you want to play shuffleboard?
I'll teach you how.
But I have to tell you I'm really
good at that," bragged Penny.
"If you'd like," said Captain Jenkins
And he chuckled to himself.
"So am I."

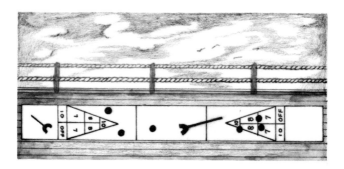

Penny and the Captain

The sun sparkled on the water.
Penny kicked off her thongs,
threw her feet up on the rail,
and said, "I'm not budging."
"Neither am I,"
said Captain Jenkins.
And they didn't move.
They sipped lemonade
with wild mint leaves.

Penny felt a cool breeze.
Darkness spread over the sky.
Great puffs of clouds rolled
in, and it began to pour.

"It's a thunderstorm!"
cried Penny. "Oh, rats!
Our whole day is spoiled."
They packed up and ran inside.

Outside the waves were high.
Drops of rain splattered the deck,
making rainbows in the puddles.
Penny tried to count them.
"What should we do now?"
wondered Penny.
"There's plenty to do,"
said Captain Jenkins.
"Let's go out in the rain."
They played hide and seek.
They blew soap bubbles.
They splashed in the puddles,
and tried to catch raindrops
in their mouths.

When they got cold,
they went in and drank
hot chocolate and apple cider
spiced with cinnamon sticks.

They read aloud to each other.
Everyone curled up and became
very sleepy, as *The Silverfish*
rocked in a gentle rhythm.

When the day was over,
Penny turned to Captain Jenkins
and sighed, "Of all the places
we've been, going nowhere was
the most tiring of all."
"I know," yawned the captain.
And they said, "Good night."

I do my thing, and you do your thing.
I am not in this world to live up to your expectations
And you are not in this world to live up to mine.
You are you and I am I,
And if by chance we find each other, it's beautiful.
If not, it can't be helped.

Fritz Perls

Jane Breskin Zalben is a painter, etcher, book designer, and a well known illustrator of children's books, both those written by herself and by others. Her beautiful illustrations for Lewis Carroll's JABBERWOCKY and Jane Yolen's AN INVITATION TO THE BUTTERFLY BALL have recently brought her particular acclaim.

A graduate of New York's High School of Music and Art and of Queens College, she pursued further studies in lithography at Pratt Graphics Center. She was an art director for a large publisher which she left in order to devote more time to her own illustration and writing. She is on the faculty of the School of Visual Arts in New York City. Ms. Zalben lives with her husband, an architect, and their small son in Port Washington, New York.

The art was prepared with a pencil, pen and 000 brush
using water colors and china ink on Opaline Parchment.
The display type is Caslon Antique. • The text type is Plantin.
The type was set at the Royal Composing Room and Cardinal Typographers.
Printed by Halliday Lithograph Corp.
Jacket printed by Phillips Offset.
Bound by The Book Press.